foc
2-

White Lie

White Lie

(stories)

Clint Burnham

anvil press • vancouver • 2021

Library and Archives Canada Cataloguing in Publication

Title: White lie / Clint Burnham.
Names: Burnham, Clint, 1962- author.
Identifiers: Canadiana 20210226978 | ISBN 9781772141740 (softcover)
Classification: LCC PS8553.U665 W55 2021 | DDC C813/.54—dc23

Cover image: Stephen Waddell, *Expulsion*, 2018
Cover design by rayola.com
Interior by HeimatHouse
Author photo by Chris Brayshaw

Represented in Canada by Publishers Group Canada
Distributed by Raincoast Books

The publisher gratefully acknowledges the financial assistance of the Canada Council for the Arts, the Canada Book Fund, and the Province of British Columbia through the B.C. Arts Council and the Book Publishing Tax Credit.

Anvil Press Publishers Inc.
P.O. Box 3008, Station Terminal
Vancouver, B.C. V6B 3X5 CANADA
www.anvilpress.com

PRINTED AND BOUND IN CANADA

this book is in memory of my mother

Table of Contents

You're Supposed to Be at the Airport!

I took the ferry over from the mainland, but it turned out I came back by plane from one harbour to another. Waiting for the plane were some university *administrators*, who were discussing learning outcomes. The floatplane held six passengers, and so I had the unfortunate destiny of hearing their mindless chatter for the entire thirty-minute trip. Neither the *aboriginal* whalers, caught in a storm, nor Spanish *sailors* fearful for their lives as they ventured into that harbour over two centuries earlier, suffered as much as I did on that March day.

Bridge

Upon returning to my hotel I immediately went out. The room was very small, although not so small that it did not include a "loft" with a bed in case I was travelling with my family, which I was not. I went out in one direction, and then returned, and inquired of the South Asian gentleman at the desk as to the best local curry shop. He pointed me in the other direction, to the same street where I'd spent some time in a pub. The bombings of July 7 had taken place up the road, but this was some years later, and there was no trace, if you did not count the hookah smokers sitting on café patios, even in January.

Artisans

He said as he sat at the table, nodding to a portrait above the archway, Who is that guy, he must be a Nazi. The other artists, none of whom were painters, and in fact considered painting to be what you gave up two weeks into art school so you could get into *digital* art or *design*, chuckled, as they were not from the city and had no allegiances or knowledge. A woman who worked at the museum, and who was paying for their dinner, looked a bit pained. Her boyfriend, who looked to be about twenty years younger than her, nonetheless was too old to sport the ponytail he still affected.

Tip (I)

This was on a bus leaving a small town in New England. He had a bag of lettuce and grapes with him, and the driver was outside having a smoke, and he was the only passenger, or, at least, he could see no other passengers from his row, about fifteen back from the front. A guy his age, but much skinnier, with short hair that hadn't been cut recently and in jeans and a T-shirt, got onto the bus and approached him and said Man, you got any money? He pulled an American five dollar bill out of his pocket and gave it to the guy, who left the bus in a hurry.

Tip (II)

In Cincinnati, he walked from the downtown hotel zone to another, more luxurious hotel near the hospital and university. On the way there, on a street called Vine, he passed a cinder block bar with the word Dive painted, dark grey on light grey. After attending some sessions and having some drinks with his friends from Québec, he took a taxi back downtown, having asked at the desk, and being directed to a large gentleman in a black leather car coat, who escorted him to an SUV with tinted windows. When he paid for the ride he dropped some money on the floor and the driver mentioned it to him, but he just scuttered into the hotel lobby.

Cool

The day before they had been in some ancient monasteries that had thick stone columns, cool in the summer heat. Eight time zones away his sister was getting married but he ended up staying at a friend's place in Colchester. The laundry machine seemed to work fine, although he had to leave his clothing hanging off the backs of chairs and windowsills to dry. A day later in Cambridge he found the poet's house, where they looked up "potted" in the dictionary, which lay on a table the back corner of which was covered in sauce bottles.

Resemblance

This was on a bus to Oregon. In the seat in front of him was a tall guy, and in the seat in front of the tall guy was a mother and her child, a boy maybe five years old. The boy kept turning around and looking at the tall guy. Finally he said, You look like Michael Jordan! The tall guy laughed, said may-be, and the mother laughed. Later he got to his destination where a friend of his, Rich, had shaved his head in solidarity with his wife, who was undergoing cancer treatment. Rich's daughter still had long hair.

Prostate Cancer Story

He was visiting a small city in the interior of the province to talk about poetry. It was November, and so he had grown a moustache, which everyone said made him look gay, and he was staying with a gay friend, and they had muesli for breakfast. His friend made very good coffee. Later, talking to his friend's poetry class, he made a joke about prostate exams, and how much he enjoyed them. His friend did not crack a smile, and he remembered that his friend was still waiting to find out if he had tenure. But in the end everything was alright, his friend got tenure, and they went out to an Italian restaurant, which was quite roomy on a Tuesday night, you had to drive through a trailer park to park.

Corner

It was a small industrial city: pulp mills, the lawyers and doctors and professors lived up the hill, away from the smell. He drove to a shopping mall and parked, waiting for his friend at the coffee shop. Others had driven two hours through blizzards for a *mocha*. Whether sitting together or alone, people wore fleece jackets zipped up, protection against blasts of air when the bell rang and the door opened. But it was sunny there, in the late afternoon, and when his friend arrived they walked for an hour down numbered streets where agencies for homeless people outnumbered functioning businesses. Wide streets, salt encrusted mounds of snow at parkade entrances. Their destination was closed, and when they returned to the parking lot it somehow only took fifteen minutes. His friend's hair was cut straight across his high forehead, and he looked like a bust of Caesar in the British Museum.

Ravine (I)

He had been down or through many ravines, remembered the gully beside his house in Arvida, the ravine where his friend Beaver tried to set a fire in northern Alberta, and the ravines in Toronto behind houses in Rosedale, where his friend, who sold his books on the street before abandoning literature for day trading, set a story about a Thoreau-like recluse who sets up camp, perhaps meeting other juvenile delinquents. This ravine ran along the rivers in Edmonton, which he did not remember from his youth there forty years earlier, having learned that whenever, as a philosopher, he returned to towns or cities he'd lived in during his youth he never had occasion to visit the old neighbourhoods, which people usually said had been taken over by native Indians anyway.

Ravine (II)

The paths along the ravine were for joggers in the summer-time and for cross-country skiers in the winter. The signs that were small maps were the same regardless, but in the winter the small rectangular holes on the posts (holes that further up were where the sign was bolted on) had light dustings of snow on their lower curve. The snow also clung to the bottom edge of the sign, adding a difficult to design effect of white shadow to the half-inch-thick border.

Cancelgar

The borscht at the small mountain town airport was quite good, which those in the know said was because of the high number of Doukhobors who had lived in the region for almost 100 years. It was not clear if they had been fleeing the Tsar or the Soviets. During the Second World War, pacifists, some elected to work on one of the large hydro-electric dams being built along the many rivers in that corner of the province, in that way, without having to shoot or be shot at, contributing to the war effort. He waited most of the afternoon for his plane to make it out, having being told by his friend, an ex-hippie who he knew from many years earlier, that he could drive him over to the next town and airport, if need be.

Unexpected

The American said *tchuss*! to him when he left the function, and, walking with some others, including a woman in furs and high heels whom his friend offered to help carry up some icy stairs, they made their way to an apartment in the district. The couple who had invited them, and who were both named Sam, had set the table, even though when the male Sam had been at the function he seemed to have invited people over on the spur of the moment. They looked at a Keith Haring painting that hung in the open format bathroom, and Sam told him and his friend that their son's wife was expecting a child. The other Sam, when Sam told her this, frowned and said that that was private information, and, although she did not say as much, he felt that he did not know them well enough to have learned of their family's latest news.

The Arge

The released prisoner whose job it was to shovel the charity shop's parking lot was doing it for the third time that day. He had a rigid curved shovel one metre wide, and the lot was big enough to hold twenty-five or thirty vehicles. There weren't that many today, as it had been snowing for three days straight. The storm had come in from Russia, bringing news as bad as anything you saw on the television. One pile of snow came up to his shoulder. He always ached there, especially when it was cold like now, from when he was arrested the last time, when he'd been driving dirty, bringing dope in from Morocco, this was when border controls were more strict. He'd been stopped in the Tyrols. The national polizei hadn't liked his attitude. Wearing sneakers with fat grey laces, he leaned into the shovel, pushing a path across where he'd shovelled at noon. He still had hours till closing time, and he heard they were tightening up the borders again. His boss came out, she had the fine-lined, leathery face of a chain smoker. He couldn't afford cigarettes any more, and she asked him to sweep the snow off her car. He shovelled away the drift behind it first.

Jars

When he left the hospital he did not want to put on a seat belt. The provincial laws had recently changed, and a shoulder strap was now required, as well as the lap belt. His father brusquely told him to do it, not to be silly. He put a pillow between the strap and his chest. When he returned home, it was bending over that was the most difficulty, that he had the most trouble with, not being sure, always wondering if everything would pop open. When he'd been in the hospital, there were two tubes coming out of the eight-inch incision across his chest, leading to two jars under the bed, which slowly filled with liquid. One jar, the larger one, contained liquid that was a brownish-red, and, the other, a smaller jar, held clear liquid. He was in the hospital for just over five days, arriving the afternoon before the operation, which itself was in the morning, when you are freshest, and leaving four days later, at around noon, although he was not very hungry when he arrived home.

Claat

She had to telephone his parents and had never met them before. The incident took place at the training base, where he was in an infantry platoon preparing to leave for Afghanistan. They had known each other briefly, and married, as both were expecting to be deployed in the near future. Because she was in the clinic when he was brought in, she knew that the problems associated with a blood clot were grave. If it moved from his leg to his brain he would suffer a stroke, which would effectively end his career. As it turned out, he was fine the next day, and they met with his parents at a nearby motel for a short wedding celebration.

Port Alberni (I)

Their truck broke down on the highway leading out of Port Alberni, and the first few vehicles that passed did not stop. But it was a warm, summer day, not too hot, which meant the wait was pleasant. A large car, a Cadillac he thought, did stop, and gave them a jump. When they returned to town they went to the Canadian Tire outlet and the mechanics were able to get to it right away. In the meantime the couple went for coffee, and then he browsed at a paperback exchange in the strip mall, finding some Elmore Leonard cowboy novels. On leaving town they meant to remember to spot the location where they'd broken down, but they forgot, and were in Ucluelet before dark.

Port Alberni (II)

Because there was a motocross event on that weekend, it was hard to get a hotel or even motel room, and the establishment they eventually found looked pretty sketchy. The child was asleep and he carried him up the stairs while she got the bags and unlocked the door. The room did not smell of cigarette smoke, although the carpeting looked like an ashtray had been dumped onto it and ground in with many boots and shoes and runners. He opened the window onto a small balcony and the view out the back, in the summer twilight, was of tall, dark trees, the conifers of the West Coast, the sky behind them. When the child awoke they went out for a bite to eat. The restaurant attached to the motel was Japanese, but most of the customers, who were all white, were drinking beer. Later that night the couple was awoken by the thumping of a bed frame hitting the wall behind them, and, even later, by a woman crying on the balcony outside.

Pemberton Loop

When they drove up by way of Boston Bar they stopped at the town where the Thompson and Fraser rivers met. Down at the river itself were piles of rocks from when the Chinese would pan for gold. They were very tidy and it looked like a beach in the city that had been organized by the parks and recreation staff. Later they went for a hike in the Stein Valley. The next morning they drove to a mud bog event on the way to Pemberton. The police were checking vehicles going down the one road to the event, looking for open containers and whatnot. In one of the last roadside stops before heading back to the coast, they bought some smoked salmon and Indian candy. This was in the mid 1990s, and the shop also sold Tupac Shakur and George Strait CDs.

Happy Hearts

The campsite was outside Tober Moray on the Bruce Peninsula in Ontario, part of the vast stretch of northern wilderness called *cottage country* because it was within a reasonable, three- or four-hour drive, for residents of Toronto who wanted to escape for a weekend vacation. They went to a café in town for breakfast a couple of times, the second time a loud-mouthed guy at the next table told his friends he liked shooting cans. When no one followed up on that he clarified: Mexi-*cans*, Jamai-*cans*, Puerto Ri-*cans,* with a loud guffaw. The woman who'd brought out their food had a long black ponytail, and had her back to the room, walking back into the kitchen. He made some kind of remark from their table, and the room went silent. Later they took a boat tour over to one of the Flowerpot islands, a power boat like Greenpeace used when they challenged Japanese whalers.

Dollar Forty-Nine Day

When they were children in the 1970s they would visit one set of grandparents in Vancouver and the other ones on Vancouver Island. If it was a Tuesday when they were there their mother would go downtown with her mother-in-law for $1.49 Day at Woodward's. You need sharp elbows, their father said, they were sitting in the backyard under the fruit trees. It was essentially a white sale. The backyard had two levels, a berm where the trees grew, and a lower level where their grandfather's garden was. The alley behind the house was steep and curved and there was so little room around the Cadillac in the garage that their grandmother had to wait until he pulled the car out before she got in. They owned two houses next to each other and when, later that decade, they tore down one to build a new one and moved into it, the real estate agent who sold the old house for them didn't tell them it was the Chinese who were moving in.

I Can't Hear You

He liked to say, I put my wallet on the table. Sometimes he would say 'Jew him down,' but this was usually when they were playing cards and had been drinking. He cheated at cards, of course, and was always peeved when he lost or was caught out. You couldn't call him on his bluffs. When they played *Rummoli* the playing cloth was soft, and furred at the folds. There was a photograph of their poodle, who was named Martini, smoking a cigarette, this was when everyone smoked. In the basement was a bar with many of the bar paraphernalia one saw in those days, a guy wrapped around a lamp-post, a sign saying I don't have a drinking problem, I get drunk, I fall down, no problem. It was all very cozy. And a player piano, which he never heard working, but he remembered it a few years later, reading Conrad's *The Secret Agent*, and the sudden noise of the player piano in the basement of the Silenus Restaurant, an anarchist hangout: *The din it raised was deafening.*

White Lie

The trip from the mainland was on a car ferry, the railings lumpy with layers of white paint over bubbles from scraped-off rust. When their car left the ferry it followed a twisting road, you might have thought the children would get car-sick from the stops and starts, the turns, the slow-downs, but the father was a careful driver, had never had a ticket. In his teens he had been a drag car racer in the delta flats and that had gotten it out of his system. At his in-laws they stayed for a few days, the grandfather frightening the youngest girl with his east coast bluster, the rocks on the beach smooth and hot in the August sun. The year before there was some confusion, a visit had been planned but suddenly put off and the in-laws had gone to Washington state that week. They later learned his wife's younger brother had been in a car accident, he wasn't driving, but he broke his leg, and for some reason his parents did not want to stay in the valley. The driver always gets off scot-free, his mother-in-law would say for years after.

Say 'Uncle'

When her parents came to visit she said to her children, Don't act as if we've never had meat before. His parents always called their margarine 'margarine,' although when they weren't there they just called it 'butter.' When the uncle visited, he had just finished putting a *faux* brick wall up in the dining alcove. He posed for a picture with the oldest girl and said, Oh sure now, with that behind me they'll think we're in the bar, won't they? When his wife died he found letters from her brother, asking for money, and he tore them up.

Abbotsford

His grandparents lived out their last years in a Mennonite nursing home, but ten years before that, when they were in their last condo, his grandfather would mutter about the Mennonites owning everything. His wife was a Mennonite, so it was awkward, not that she cared. A couple of decades before that, his uncle, their son, made a living buying furniture made by Mennonites in Mexico and bringing it up to Canada to sell for a profit. When they moved into the nursing home he cleaned out their place, the opera records, a Hasselblad camera, wood carving tools, kitchenware, furniture they still owed money on, memorabilia from a trip to Pennsylvania in the late 1990s when he surprised his brother he had not seen for better than forty years, and put the lot on the *Burnaby Bidding Wars* group on Facebook, even though at that time he was living in Clearbrook and it was a hassle, many trips to Lougheed Mall or Metrotown to deliver the goods. All told he made probably nine hundred, a thousand clear, if you didn't count the gas and his time.

Short Story Long Title

Long story short it should not take more than six seconds give or take to read slash write this.

Harlem Gentrifixer

Truth was he was a bit of a "go everywhere" kind of guy but he had a brownstone a couple of blocks north of 110th and ran it on Airbnb. Mexican guy was live-in in the basement and ran the towels and linens through the laundry between drop-ins, made sure the Wi-Fi worked, that kind of shit. The wine store down the street had regular Friday nights now and the coffee shop on the boulevard does a sick pour-over. There's only one guy sleeping on the street now, but he's a vet, so.

Smartphone Or Book?

What do you read on the subway? Take one or the other out of your pocket. A third option, the throw-away commuter paper with this week's terrorist story and this week's celeb exposé. All newspapers are throwaway unless you're the guy with a bag of them on the train, room with stacks like furniture, regular *Zeitungesser* in the café. Fibs all round. Finish writing this in your notebook before you reach your stop at the end of the line then hope you can read your drunken handwriting.

My Story Is a Photograph

PHOTO-STYLE FRAMING: Each story is contained within a single page. One cannot help but think that there is a request being made: Read as you would see or look at an image or photo. Survey the (document/)content(/"evidence"); supply any necessary extrapolation.

iPad Mini

for Stuart "Pods" Ross

The poet wanted to know how he could get his cow video off his iPad mini onto his laptop. He did not have the Lion operating system, he had Tiger. One friend suggested — the poet asked the cloud, or crowd, or hive, on Facebook — one person suggested emailing it to himself. Also it was too big a file to email, even to himself. Someone else suggested iCloud, and he reported back (over ten people had piped up by now) he was registering for iCloud. Then the thread disappeared and I tried asking the poet but he never got back to me.

Positive Statement

He picked them up at the airport, there were two levels for cars, one for arrivals and one for departures. His son was flying in his uniform and he put his cap on the dashboard in case the police were running road checks, which he was not very happy about. Later, when they moved into the military housing, she said, just let me get the drapes up, for privacy, that would always be her first priority. The boy bragged to his friends about his father's rank, which his brother heard, and told their parents, thinking it was a problem, but he was wrong, they didn't care, subscribing to the *shoot the messenger* school of thought.

Can You Email It To Me? (I)

After making sure the text was now no longer *bold*, which entailed hitting the control-I combination, but before that, she had made a new page, which meant bringing the *cursor* up to the top of the screen and touching first *Insert* and then usually, even though *Break* was the first option, she might go all the way down the *Menu* to *Footnote* or even *Symbol*, for sometimes she had to insert foreign words with foreign diacritics, before *scrolling* or just *sliding* back up to *Break* and then *Page break*. She tried to remember what the verb, if there was a verb, a user function, for what you did with the *cursor*, rubbing her forefinger on the *mousepad* as it moved around the screen or a *drop-down menu*, and if the italicized words would look like what one used to call *hyperlinks*. Just forward it. Click on the link. Unknown user.

Can You Email It To Me? (II)

Standing outside a *vernissage*, discussing her day's work after telling a very forward guy who grew up in Kenya so didn't have the usual regional British accent, You can, but just a bit, you're not allowed to bite. She wanted to do some more work that night and the other guy, a painter, said, yeah, holding his beer bottle and cigarette in his left hand, *do some more work*, holding an imaginary brush in his right hand, then squinting, which he had to do anyway from the cigarette smoke now that the cigarette was in his mouth, squinting as if looking at the canvas with the brush held up for scale.

The Number You Are Calling Is Not In Service

Because no one had business cards anymore the way to get in contact was either to connect up right away on Facebook or exchange numbers on your phones. She wasn't on Facebook so Mary asked Helga if she would connect them but first of all she had to make sure she had Helga's number even though they're friends on Facebook. Helga gave her her number and she tried it, meaning to text her, but called her and got a Not in Service message just as Helga said no, that was a mistake. That's the wrong number, sorry, I gave you, that was my old landline. This time Mary texted her saying Hi it's Mary do you have Serena's number but Helga was scrolling through her contacts, she had a Samsung, Mary still liked her Blackberry even though it wasn't owned in Canada anymore but the technology was Canadian, she had worked on some of the architecture when she was at Waterloo. Instead of texting back, Helga, after scrolling, just told Mary Serena's number.

Rap?Sure!

In the spring of 1981 he was in the navy hospital at Esquimault, he had kidney stones. He had Blondie's album at home but not in the barracks. Once a band came and played for a Friday night and did the B-52s' "Rock Lobster." A couple of years earlier, waiting for transport home, sitting in the corridor on the floor, holding the Clash's *Give'em Enough Rope* he bought at a record store in Edmonton, a female corporal asking him about it. Now, some of the other guys on the ward were in for vasectomies, two or three of them, and a guy with a G4O4 with a metal structure around his head. The nurse when she was folding his clothes for his suitcase, she knew how to roll them up, kept up the chatter, was singing the Blondie song "Rapture" she told him he looked like he was *from Mars, eating cars,* trying to cheer him up, the curved pads with foam on his shoulders, wing nuts at the top of the bars that held the braces on his forehead. But for his kidney stones, our story's hero just had to measure his fluid intake and his urine every day, filter it, he was in the hospital b/c he fainted taking a leak, probably passed the stone then, they said when they released him.

Officer of the Day
(abandoned)

He was on spaz parade.

White dubbin on gaiters. Knee pad jokes. Officer of the day.

Corrections

It was a Sony Xperia, not a Samsung. C&A refers to "coats and 'ats", not "Coats and Hats." The grey border should be taken out. It ends Sprechen sie Deutsch baby, not Aufeidesein baby, which isn't how you spell it and isn't the end anyway. Achtung Nazis are around. We misspelled the surname of the film actor Seth Rogan as Seth Rogen in a piece about the UK launch of *The Interview*, a comedy about two hapless US journalists' attempts to assassinate the North Korean leader Kim Jong-un (Full cinematic release for *The Interview*, but little publicity as movie heads for UK). A formatting problem gave the wrong meaning to a sentence about the Big Bang which said: "At first the universe was inconceivably tiny but then approximately 10-37 seconds into the expansion, something called cosmic inflation led to exponential growth and the seeds of what we observe today." The writer intended that to be 10^{-37} — a tiny fraction of one second (Is time, after all, real? Two mavericks take an axe to the established theories of cosmology). (No spelling suggestions.)

Belief

He kicked her between the legs and left her outside his door. Two or three days later he was out on bail and asked me for a letter. I asked him what for and he said it was for the hearing. I phoned his lawyer but his lawyer wouldn't tell me if he was his lawyer or not. When I complained to my boss about this she said they can't. The next week I saw him he brought a letter from his lawyer, it was printed out from a dot-matrix printer, the edges of the pages were a bit shredded from where the tractor rolls had been ripped off. That Christmas I gave him some socks for him and his son. When I'd see him again over the years, he grew a beard, it was curly and white, giving him a Santa with a jutting jaw look.

A Clean Gore-Tex Jacket

She was the prostitute who gave him cheap yellow sunglasses for his baby son. The bus strike was on then so they had the graduation ceremony in a brand new building in the neighbourhood, he wore the closest thing he had to a suit, which he'd bought at a thrift store, no probably a vintage store, if you know the difference. When a reporter came to their class she wrote that people wore clothing from the thrift store, but most of them wore cast-offs from clothing people dumped in garbage bags at the women's shelter. Some of the teachers, who were students at the university, wore thrift store clothing because that was where you found shirts with logos for spark plugs or a name in an oval patch. There was this one guy, Randy, always had a clean, green, Gore-Tex jacket on but he kept having seizures and couldn't finish the program.

The Famous Architect

She was a graduate student at the university. There was a meeting at the anthropology museum to decide how to run a program for poor people. Students had come up with the idea and one of their professors, who was also the director of the museum, offered the board room. It was a very nice room, the building had been designed by a famous Canadian architect, at the time the most famous architect in the country. When she sat next to the director, not knowing who he was, she said that she felt as if it was a building full of looted artifacts. The brass from a *punitive British expedition* to Benin City in the 1890s. Totems from up the coast that had once *rotted* in the rich sea air, and now were dry, *desiccated*, in the climate-controlled atrium. A sculpture made from guns turned in during an *amnesty* in Mozambique. She became quite good friends with the museum director, as it turned out, and he gave her pertinent advice on setting up discussion groups in her class. *This is not kindergarten*, he said, *they do not choose who to sit with.*

Bus Tickets

A visiting dignitary from New York was in town, and visited the class for poor people, and commented that the students did not seem poor enough to him. This was said at dinner. Earlier, the students had their dinner, which was lasagna, vegetarian or not, served from large trays covered in foil so it would not lose its heat as a woman in whites, her hair in a hairnet, black and white houndstooth pants, rolled the trolley down the sidewalk from the kitchen. One of the students, Mike, slept under a truck, and would bury his tools at night so they wouldn't get stolen. Of course, he forgot one night where he had buried them, and so he never found them. His abiding interest was in earthquakes, and to see the Mars Rover. The images of the Rover that had come from so far away. The visiting dignitary was on the heli-jet the next morning going to the provincial capital with the university president, and he said that it was too bad one or two of the students could not come over with them, so the legislators could see what good work their money was doing.

The Prophet

He was writing an article about a media prophet. He would not be writing, would be taking a break, watching a TV show he had downloaded illegally, and then an idea would come into his head, *would just pop into his head* was how he would think of it. A germ of an idea for his essay, and he would pause the show, reduce the screen, and open a new document, or perhaps one that was called *Notes for essay*, and he would put down the beginning of the idea, or its germ, he wasn't sure what the metaphor would be, if the idea was a virus that spread from word to work as he wrote, or if it was *in his brain* and his writing was *working on his brain*, making the idea take form. He would pause for a minute, his left hand on the keyboard, chin and face resting on his right hand, then finish the sentence, and add a period.

Marguerite

His essay progressed or at least changed in this way. After reading a number of articles and books he began to write. But this is misleading. He always started too soon — would be reading an article and stop, put the book down, go to the kitchen table where the laptop was, and start writing. Or take a few pages of notes in his notebook. Either a small, 3x5" notebook, or the larger, 5x8" one. If he was on the computer — he read a biography of Derrida where it said the French philosopher worked in this way, and envied his wife, Marguerite, because she could just sit down and enjoy a novel, but he, Derrida, could not read without starting to write. This was a comfort, almost inordinately so, for a few days or weeks, but then the comfort faded.

For Example

Even though he wanted to write about the media prophet he did not want to write about the media itself, and rehearsed different ways of arguing or, really, justifying or rationalizing, why he did not. But as the time he spent on the essay continued, he realized that he was going to write about the media itself. That it would make the paper richer. He left in the rationalizations and justifications for why he did not necessarily have to write about the media, however, like the slice of lemon that adds a tartness to an otherwise heavy slab of salmon.

billeh via fb

The most irritating woman ever playing "Would You Rather" in the coffee shop just asked her friend if she'd rather change her last name to "Hitler" or never eat chocolate again. I would rather she left and had to BOTH change her name to "Hitler" and never have chocolate again. I would also rather she had to finish all my marking, and get audited by Revenue Canada.

My Practice

What he would do was to write four or five of the stories —
he still thought of them as photographs that developed over
time — in a morning or afternoon. He would then collect
them into a document and make the Word document into
a PDF. Then he would put the PDF into the cloud. Actually,
when he made it into a PDF he put it into the cloud at the
same time. This was on the laptop. Then, on his tablet, he
opened the PDF in the PDF reading program. As each page
scrolled by, he took a picture of it with the tablet itself —
from the screen. He then opened the camera program,
looked at the pictures of the stories, and if he was happy
with them he put them onto the internet, in this way publishing photographs of his stories. Or put them *back* onto
the internet, he corrected himself, for they had already been
on the internet when they were in the cloud. But then the
stories were private, or at least as private as things are in the
cloud, and now they were public. Or at least...

An Imbroglio

Initially when the poets met they talked about Elmore Leonard, especially about his Florida novels. Then they started going to the track, once one of them found a *Kraftwerk* album at a yard sale on the way, and ended up carrying a 12-inch of *Autobahn* for the rest of the afternoon, walking along Pender and then Hastings, going into the stands, getting a beer, placing some bets at the window, going outside and watching the horses run, going to the urinals, all the way until getting home eight or nine hours later, flushed and sweaty, hot. It was a hot August afternoon, *The Racing Form* crumpled against a record album. A couple of weeks later there was a fight outside a poetry reading, one of the poets attacking another, thinking it was someone who was not there. There was a professor in attendance as well, and he worried what the people from out of town would think. Others worried about the poet who was attacked, and still others worried about the one who did the attacking. It is even possible, he thought, that he will attack me for writing this now.

High Noon

She liked to play Kruder and Dorfmeister when she was painting on a Saturday afternoon cuz she knew they used to live in the building. She wore a white Tyvek suit, white trainers with Velcro straps that she wore all the time, her dark curly hair and a big fuzzy black hat because the heating was never on. Rolling sideways, for some reason that worked better for her than up and down, then the paint dripped or dried against the action, she said but it didn't really move all that much. She used to gesso the canvases in the winter, figuring all the movement she had to do was enough to keep her warm but she was wrong, not about getting warm, she got warm, but the gesso separated, the layers between, so it cracked, and she had to start over again, which entailed a degree of organization she wasn't that happy about, making sure she had enough canvases prepped and stretched before it got cold. No, that was wrong, strike that, she didn't use to gesso the canvases, she only did it once.

American Girl

When he is laughing in the wine bar I look in the mirror to better see his eyes close and mouth (surrounded by a greying goatee) open. Then he coughs, a bit liquidly. He has dotted tattoos around his neck, with an open space at the front for his Adam's apple and at the back for his spine, the same pattern on the backs of his hands. A sliver necklace and a V-neck sweater. When he gets home, it is still light out but he is fairly drunk. The staircase is littered with energy drink cans and sticker wrappers from the neighbourhood grocery store. He is going to catch some Zs before going out. He bought a balloon and a doll for his niece's birthday that they were celebrating in the bar. You know, he likes kids, but those ones upstairs have been bouncing a ball on the ceiling, his ceiling, their floor, for it seems like hours now, and that's really the last straw.

Space Cadet

Before they left he told the boys not to wear jeans, to wear corduroy. Denim sucked up the damp from the snow, stayed wet for days, chafed your crotch like nobody's business. An old woman did the cooking for them, she was Cree from Marie Lake, but more to the point, two of her grandsons were in the camp. This was to *straighten them out*, she would say as she tapped a hardboiled egg against the counter to peel it, they can't get into trouble *if they have to keep busy*. When Donald fell asleep, one of the bigger boys put his wrist into a can of water. The broad can that Safeway jam came in. The idea being it would make you piss your sleeping bag. He had glasses that were tinted, so it looked as though he had eye shadow on, and he had a David Bowie cassette, so that was enough to tip the scale. After a day of learning how to set a rabbit snare and build a lean-to and ice fish and capture the flag, they leg wrestled in the large room.

Is This Place Taken?

When the philosopher, who taught books by Nietzsche, Dostoeveski, and Sartre, and who would lock the door once class began, to keep out the laggards, boarded the bus after work, she usually sat in the first seat to the left of the back door. It was an articulated bus that made a ten-minute shuttle run to the train station, so she knew the three or four buses very well, the advertisements for family planning and children's TV and cellphone providers, the blue cushion on one of the buses that was raised a bit, as if it were a Chesterfield and someone had just been looking for coins between the cushions. After this homey atmosphere the train was more hectic, suburbanites going to a hockey game and unsure of their stop, gaggles of girls with their arms locked, blocking the centre aisle, sometimes an old man who would change seats *deliberately*.

A Ringer

Because the buildings were mostly five or six storeys in height, the sun rarely hit the sidewalks in the winter. The American city-style grid between the subway stop and the hospital was four blocks wide, running from east to west, and he frequently forgot which direction led to the city centre, which way was north, which way led to the forest. When he looked out one window it was to the west, and sunny, if it was sunny, and through the others it was to the east. The top two floors of the building between his flat and the hospital had a glassed-in corridor, and sometimes at night two or three windows would light up at once, as if by magic, the magic of electricity. Truth be told, it was the last neighbourhood in the city to have electricity connections, and workers would share beds, a practice known as *hot-sheeting* because the linen never got a chance to cool.

Yashica

Before there was a point-and-shoot there was an SLR, a single lens reflex camera. But the *Yashica* was what he purchased at the American PX at the base in West Germany near Baden, that was where you got all the bargains, and many of the young airmen also bought stereo components there. But he was a family man, and contented himself with a 35 mm camera, and a *Blaupunkt* radio, which also, he learned when he returned to Canadian soil, picked up TV signals. It was a radio you could install in your car, although he never did that, and it had a handle across the top that folded back.

Like a Motherfucker

How can you tell if someone's looking at you, he wondered. That I've never been able to figure out. *A 500 yard stare*, a friend of his described it, but who can see that far? The person walking by on the sidewalk, he looks at her but her eyes point straight forward, fixedly, as if she were told to do so, if you could say that eyes point anywhere, but people do anyway, don't they?

Selfie-ish

A selfie with the Odessa steps behind her, the woman not yet shot and the baby carriage not yet tumbling. A selfie with Liberty leading the people behind her. A selfie with the death of Marat behind her. A selfie with Plato, Aristotle, and Socrates walking behind her, as glorious and beautiful as the women on the beach in Proust. A selfie with the protests at Maidan, Ukraine, behind her. A selfie with *Guernica* behind her, just about to be covered up for the Secretary's address. A selfie with her sister behind her, holding up her phone, showing the temperature *feels like* -51 degrees. A selfie with *Batman* playing behind her on a large monitor in a gallery, it's from the 1960s TV show, and it's cut so you only ever see Robin.

Some Objects

Photographs from memory. Coffee grounds in the sink, black grains wet against grey aluminum. A Korean or Japanese sauce bottle lying on its back on a striped red and white tablecloth, the stripes diagonal. Men working with their shirts off, planing a floor, light coming in the window behind them on a *dust jacket*, in a painting on a *book jacket*, sunlight on the table next to the book and the envelope it arrived in. Two children, one on the other's lap, a slice of bacon on the plate in front of them, an open safety gate and stairwell behind them. A bag of chips. A hat. The same hat. The same hat a third time, from another point of view.

Mask

Years earlier, he was riding his bike home from downtown, on Main Street, a copy of the novel bungee strapped to the back. Guy at the corner asked if he'd seen the movie, said Yeah, asked if it was good, Yeah, y'know, it's Spike. Now he thinks about but can't remember if it's in the book or Harvey Keitel's character sleeps with a mask, across the river from New York, apart from his kids. Like a kid he watches TV on his computer until 1 or 2, then reads to clear his mind, sleeps, wakes up at 6 or 6:30 when the construction starts next door — a high-pitched saw, concrete cutter, or suchlike, the light coming in the window that doesn't have blinds, puts on a sleeping mask, earplugs.

C – B –

On Valentine's Day, the Kindergarten still has pictures of snow on the north side windows, and farm animals on the east. One of the animals is a donkey or an ass, hay in front if it, 5-6 yellow dots between the donkey's mouth and the hay, similar amount of dots — circles, really, an inch or two across, yellow, coming out of the other end, a haystack below it. As if the hay had not changed during its travel through the donkey. On the same block, further west and on the corner on the north side of the street, or just before the corner, was a brothel, its doorway lit in red light, hearts — they were there year 'round — on the window, a red *OPEN* sign. A large wool or fabric blanket hung over the door, for privacy, I suppose, although restaurants in the more posh parts of town had similar draperies on the inside of the doorway, to cut the draft, in the winter. Early one afternoon, as I walked away from the brothel, two girls passed me, cute, bare legs in the winter chill, coming from the subway. I didn't turn to see if they entered.

Red Tents

He was at the medical table at the squat, and a teenaged girl came up and talked to the woman next to him. Both females were from Calgary. The girl was white, maybe 15 or 16, and she'd dropped out of school, nothing was going on. Guy came up, he was out of it, drunk or something more fucked up. He said to the young girl, Go down to the corner and make me some money! He said to her, Go back to school! The older woman also from Calgary didn't say anything. No, she said, is that. She said, hey now.

How – S

He did it all for his sister, and that is super creepy, which, itself, it being super creepy, is creepy. That we think him doing it for his sister is creepy is also creepy. The client from hell. A crack in super thick glass. An elevator that maybe doesn't work anymore? Risers you'll trip on as they spiral. She really had to go. The grand piano, a data projector, planter brought in for the winter, or *from* the winter, a small Christmas wreath, photographs in which a dog slept under a picture of a dog, a child in a toy car next to rusted auto bodies, yellow-ish brown paintings. He bought her a bottle of Juniper gin, went on a date with her friend, she cried when he joined the army, emptying a waste basket that was already empty.

The Professor

She sat in the courtroom that had been designed for a terrorist trial, with bomb-proof glass between the gallery and where the defendants sat. The trial would be for five men accused of gangsterism and murder in a different city. She specialized in the literature of the ethnic or national group from which their alleged gang took its name, she did not know if that was relevant. Lunch was from Subway. They each had a different lawyer, and the one who questioned her had a large diamond earring and his hair was streaked. One of the defendants wore a very crumpled shirt, with white stripes, the sheriff had accidentally on purpose balled it up. She was not one of the chosen ones.

Is There Another Story to Type Out?

No. Not yet.

Workshop

The smell of shit was still there behind the industrial cleaner, like brushing your teeth if you have halitosis, it doesn't help. There was no privacy, all the inmates' rooms behind shatterproof glass that started three feet up the walls, none of the doors locked. No secrets. In the basement was the workshop, tools blunted from years of use but also for safety, like children's hammers and saws that can't pound or cut anything, a typewriter with its ribbon worn out of ink, any writing on the sheets of paper taken from office waste baskets.

Carnival vs Lent

I was halfway through the beer when my son pointed out it was alcohol free. Now I had a conundrum. Should I keep drinking it? So as not to waste any. Or should I just leave it and crack a real beer? I know the answer now, the next day, listening to a tea kettle rattle on the hob, leaning back, the beer can still visible on the counter, behind half a banana.

Doggie

When the temperatures hover between a few above and a few below zero Centigrade, it is the most treacherous. Some use Tiroler poles, with slung back tabs at the bottom you'd hardly think they'd have any traction, and mostly folks with them are just truckin' down the sidewalk. Or they walk their dogs, a brace of Greyhounds in *fleece jackets*, perchance. He wore cleats that, mounted on stretchy silicone of the type people wore around their wrists in the Aughts as bracelets to support Lance Armstrong's battle with prostate cancer (*LOL*), but bit into the ice with an unfazing grip, and yet did nothing to help him when he strayed off the hiking path and fell into a tree well. Shivering, at the brink of death, a short walk and car drive from *Tim Hortons*, gas stations, and ATMs, he was found by search and rescue only because of the faltering flicker of his cellphone flashlight.

Pennysaver

The man in zip-off cargo pants, but zipped, sat with his legs spread, sideways on a chair, facing the man next to him. They both had bald spots the circumference of a circle made by thumb and forefinger brought together for "OK."

Selfie in a Convex Mirror

Watch it with the selfie stick, you'll put an eye out. It's actually on a bulging convex piece of wood, and smaller than you'd think, and there's a number for it if you want to listen to a description in Italian, German, French, or English, though now you have to carry it around like a big flip phone, circa 1998, if you can believe it. His hand at the bottom swollen as if suffering from one of those medieval diseases you get from an infection, an Ebola embargo, an anti-vaxxer.

He Dressed like a Serbian Pimp

I talked him down from eight euros to three, because that was what I had in my pocket. I'd spent the rest of the five on a bottle of wine. He walked to the corner of the platz, next to a plaque honouring a general, or a Jew. Dug into the cracks in between and pulled it out, wrapped in cellophane. Down the street they test your drugs for you, text you the results if you can't wait around, posters for club kids, ravers, junkies. A Chinese guy comes up to me, says something, I can't understand him, nor he me.

Inferno I

I parked at the far corner of the lot so no one'd disturb her as she slept. The way was treacherous, salty, slimy, mounds where plows and shovels'd cleared paths for four-by-fours and subcompacts but not, it seems, a lonely traveller, yearning for the feeble glow of the VLTs and the hard choices of the mistress I never abandon.

Inferno II

I gave Joe Dante my memory stick, 32 GB, and asked him if he'd download some of his movies for me. *Maybe the entire catalogue?* That's not the same as watching them, he warned me. The whole question of why he was never nominated for an Oscar. It's cuz of the Jews, he said, they control Hollywood, and Jimmy the Greek, he runs the book. So sue me, I'm fucked.

Sometimes Always Never

He wore a Donegal tweed jacket, only the top button buttoned, to meet an Irish artist. He didn't have very good directions, so he got off the subway, went past the Starbucks and the hippie store, turned right, a bearded guy riding his bike with two kids in the cargo bucket in front approached him. He turned left — down a street he would visit twice, five minutes later — turned left again, and reached the square the artist's studio is located on. Continuing, he looked for the street numbers but they were too big. He turned left again at the next two corners, now between a small playground and the street number he wanted. He rushed with relief, having described in his locomotion a Smithson *Spiral Jetty*-like spiral, but —

Das Mrs. Sporty

Her mouth drew in on itself, tight, a Ziploc bag enclosure. He walked away, laughing, said to his buddy, "teenaged girls."

White Sites

They started with raki served with fruit plate, then feta and cukes. The first song on electric violin & keyboards was the theme from *The Godfather*. Everyone else was drinking rye & coke, heart-shaped faces, smoking furiously. The chef does vocals over the keyboard and the violinist smokes as he checks his phone for texts. A white guy, the owner, he puts a British pop show on between sets and working off a drug debt. They take pictures *to put on face-uh buk-uh*. If you order scotch you get a tray of drinks. If you order raki you get cheese but no tray. When the violinist made it squeal like a little girl, there's a frog at the end of the bow, but he's not holding it, the bro's totally laughed. Guy on the oudze reached up to scratch his nose, take a drag off his cig, talk to the bartender vocalist sitting at the next table. LED lights around the mirror behind the band give his selfie a greenish, submarine, or aquarium green glow.

Creative Writing
(theory monger)

A group of American creative writing instructors were visiting the college, and he was giving them the gears. Eh, we're just a bunch a hicks, yup, don't you start on that theory guff with us, we gotta, why they're not even, none uh them even have a flannel shirt. Then they went to the pub — it was just the student cafeteria after 4, right? — and he still wouldn't let up. That night he saw an ad on TV for a steam iron slash pickup truck, *Ladies, this will guaran-tee your hubbies will do the ironing* — in a sort of Cal Worthington schtick, the brand was Charlie Rich meets Johnny Cash. He always thought his grandfather looked like Cash.

The Human Shield

Although they never met, Caravaggio and Rubens had a bit of a competition going on. In sum, they were rivals. Rubens (1577-1640) gets to the coffee shop and orders a Nescafe — he had done some work in Iraq, trying to negotiate a treaty, did some quick portraits of Nouri al-Maliki — was surprised to discover Tang and Nescafe were so popular. This was just at the start of the *Nespresso* hegemon. Caravaggio (Milan 1573 - Porto Ercole 1610) posted a pic on Facebook, of his sketch for a new shield, with the head of the Medusa. Rubens thought he did him one better, with an entire picture, but everyone knows that when you have to outsource your snakes, it's game over.

Roman Idol

It was in a small bar in a rough part of town. Port side, near the hostel for destitute sailors, which had computers set up so melancholy Filipinos, crew members for the tankers bobbing in the harbour, could Skype home. The bar had an *American Idol*-type thing going. It was down to two final contestants, Paolo, a construction worker who still lived with his mother but did killer arias, and this satirical guy, Marcel, who did Kenny Rogers. Paolo won, and that's all she wrote.

Unintended Consequences of the 1993 Mafia Car Bomb

You wouldn't think a man my age could still be embarrassed, would you? I was going through security and kept setting it off. First my money belt, which was rather delicate, pulling it out of my *boxer-briefs*. At least I wore it on the front. And placed it on the conveyor belt. Then my watch, reading glasses, and wedding ring. Finally a pen knife, which I'd forgotten about entirely.

L.D.

The dressmaker's form in the corner of the room wore a
scarf with the same Turkish pattern you see on coffee cups,
ceilings of restaurants, notepaper. The beds were split, two
mattresses, the frames tied together with a shoe string in a
bow for quick release. A Venetian chandelier, like her ear-
rings, copying Bohemian crystal from two centuries back,
when she'd rather live here than at home, the Empress *Sisi*,
always on the move, the Olivia Newton-John of her day.

Half-dead Admiral

At the Queen's Head in Esquimalt. Gratis WLAN! The traffic's a bit hairy on a Friday afternoon — the Colwood crawl. When the mess hall ladies were on strike they set up a picket outside of Royal Roads Military College but did not interfere with our coming and going. A few years later, after work, we went to Coffee Mac's, on the Gorge, for coffee and potato skins, and he ordered apple pie. The waitress said, D'you want cheddar cheese with that dear? He did, and when it came it was a Kraft individual slice, still in its wrapper.

Susanna and the Elders

Michael was a painter, a baby boomer, draft dodger. Had a story about coming up to Canada where he told the border guy he was coming up for hunting season and the guy didn't buy it, asked what animal, let him in anyways. Michael did a painting about it some fifteen years later. Duck season or rabbit season. Riffing off the old *Bugs Bunny* routine. His apartment was full of kitsch, retro toys, over-decorated Fiesta-ware, and his paintings were jammed with icons, he admired Sue Coe, was the first person anyone knew in the 80s who was into Jim Thompson, the *Black Lizard* paperback reprints, David Goodis. When the paint store on Fort Street became an aerobics club they had to frost the glass in the front window because old men would stand there watching. But before they did that, he got a good painting out of the spectacle.

Madonna del Latte

Wendy was the best poet of their generation. Her Stevie Smith pastiches, strung together images from thrift store finds and overgrown gardens, were published in a handsome edition by a respected avant-garde press down east. Her mother drove a red 1970 Vauxhall Viva with a *Buy British* bumpersticker — another from a campaign to ban leg-hold traps. She didn't have any turn signals and had to put her right foot into a bread bag when it rained, the floorboards were so rusted. The revelations that came forward would shatter the family, although if you took the long view (and yet who can take a long view of one's own *nearest and dearest?*), one would perforce admit that there is no family without such a crime, or stain, in its branches.

Matthew

One of the apostles of the short-lived *Fernwood* scene, he started the magazine *Random Thought* (the name came from an Alexander Pope quote he found in another magazine) in the mid part of the decade, featuring Bob's Your Uncle and other local acts on its cover, exhaustively documenting in a three-part series alternative bands, plus theatre, sociology of the beach. Bring on the nubiles, he would say, quoting a British post-punk song. Better than a decade later, he washed up on the shores of the great city down the coast, putting his scrivening to work describing the artists clustered in an old industrial neighbourhood, now polluted with live-work lofts where lawyers play at being photographers.

King Solomon

Jim was a rough, acerbic, Glaswegian, a fine painter, who ran a falafel shop and left his wife for a girl half his age. He celebrated Hogmanay, the Scottish New Year's Day tradition of *first-footing*, and later, in his studio in Fan Tan Alley, in Chinatown, was found dead, a cup of broth at his side, a colour guide to mushrooms of the Pacific Northwest cracked open.

Clint

While thought by some to be good-looking, he had married young, his way out of the Jehovah's Witnesses. He now languished in the music production business (this was before the Gnutella disaster). He left the marriage before he hit twenty-five and, trading on his smouldering, *matinee-idol* looks, fled the city for California, where he shacked up with an opera singer, maintaining, via the deception common to the *dot-com* entrepreneur, the fiction of a Canadian address, the better to maintain his street cred on the local scene.

Can-Con

Connie taught literature at the university, suffered a blus-
tering Southern writer of a husband who wrote about fat
women and Shakespeare's pets, and wore scarves as only
Parisian women of a certain age can stylishly do. Yet she
did as well. She invited students to her house and unwisely
served red wine (white carpet, beige sofa). Her husband
once read a poem at the local gallery that began "Is it in yet?
God *damn* it, of course it is!" and she held her wine glass in
one hand, her elbow in the other, her lips pursed, but then
relaxed, recalling the advice on wrinkles in *Chatelaine*.

Queen of the Scene

Other women deferred to her, and she had that hauteur which only comes with being a diplomat's wife and writing poems about secretaries and the kind of ski lifts they had before Whistler became a theme park.

Bosch Fan Fiction (I)

Jerry had an open house that day, and so he wasn't answering his pager. A guy came in twice a year from Hong Kong and you met him in a hotel room, he measured you, three weeks later the suit arrived in a big FedEx box. The next morning, he met with Harry and the case was nothing, why he bothered, Jerry didn't know. He told his wife he was going to the BPO that night, the Black Police Officers association, gave Harry a heads-up on the odd chance she phoned in. He was glad, when they came around to ask about making a TV series, that there'd be more brothers in the cast. He knew it was hopeless, tryna put the LAPD in a positive light for most of South Central, but you could always try. Simi Valley, though, who knew he'd sell so many up there? You never can tell.

Bosch Fan Fiction (II)

"Money" Chandler did better in the TV series than she did in real life, where she was offed by a serial killer, you never saw so many serial killers as you did on cop shows, but she wasn't really bothered by their inaccuracy. For women, the thing was, you couldn't win, you were either a "man eater-upper," as Chris Penn said, memorably, or you were just arm candy. She was neither, really, just a damn good lawyer who did what lawyers were supposed to do: defend their client. She knew, that soon as a cop was up on some trumped-up charges — *never trust cops investigating cops* — they'd come crawling.

Bosch Fan Fiction (III)

He was named for the painter, Hieronymus Bosch, muddy brown and red scenes of devils with bird legs, men pooping out of upper storey windows, he never knew where his mother got interested in paintings, but he knew what he'd seen in his life on the Hollywood pavement was weirder, more soul-destroying than any old master painting. He had looked into the eyes of murderers, of men and women who had no humanity left in them, and if he ever wondered if that destroyed him as well, he tried to salve his soul with dollops of jazz, Eric Dolphy or Errol Garner, a bottle or six of beer, his cantilevered house, high above the Paramount lights.

Hundred-year-old Internet Café

He expected Dante's or Pound's or at least Lowry's medieval Italy, but got, instead, upset at bastardized English in the Food Rock Café, and mattress ads as if the world were a book with fingers hooked into it like bookmarks. Bookmarks he could clear faster than a browser history of a Russian writer machine-gunning a city, a Serbian poet on the phone nearby. Dante was non-union, celebrating, in *Paradiso*, blood filling the Marseilles harbour, Falco, not the 80s troubadour but the Dick Cheney of the 13th century, urging yet another invasion.

Pull the Choke

First he sent him a link, the subject line read *Against Humanity*, it was a link to a story on a Greek novelist on Arts and Letters Daily. This was before twitter, before aggregators, before things went viral. They started hanging out, looking at videos of suicide bombers while the girlfriends talked about their birds. They had a kid and they'd bring it along or he'd come by with it in a backpack purpose-built, once it almost fell over on the lawn, in a pizza joint on Broadway. The girl at the counter told him not to drink with his kid on his back, another time a woman asked him Did you put sunscreen on your child?

Trustfundfanfiqista

He drove to school, taught his class, drove home, she was at work, he drove out to pick her up. She was still busy for another hour or two — it was after midnight. The company had left Quebec during the Anglo capital flight in the late 70s, its name invented so it didn't have to be made Francophone. He was working on a story about Steve McGarrett and "Danno," a wedding in Hawaii, after spending Xmas in Waikiki, the Japanese food there was delish.

Duffle (I)

Before he joined up, he'd had an older kit bag, thick dark khaki, it was a tube that opened on the top with a U-shaped hasp that slipped into brass ovals. Then you put your lock onto it, there was a strap and you could carry it slung over your shoulder. When he joined up, the bag had been updated, now a lighter shade of canvas, and opened down its length, closed by a zipper and four or five large buttons. You could fit more into the older design, more tube socks and wife beaters, the newer one was more formless and harder to pack tight as a nun's cunt, which was what your tie knot was supposed to be, anyway. The newer duffle bag had two straps, for carrying, but they fit awkwardly on your shoulders, the top flopping over and pushing your head forward.

Duffle (II)

After he left the Forces, he took his laundry in his kit bag to the laundromat on Quadra Street. Kitty-corner to the Safeway, where his friend Ken worked, once, when a guy parked in the handicapped spot he asked him what his handicap was. *The Gods Must Be Crazy* played for two or three years at the movie theatre there. His basement apartment was on Empress, and between his bed and the doorway he placed his barracks box, on which he often barked his shin.

Favouritism

The bar was called Felicita's and was named for a Portuguese woman who had worked as a cleaner in the building for the previous decade. You could NOT use SOS-type pads to clean the grill. They were forbidden by the health regulations, but when John Graham (then active in the anti-apartheid movement, now a lobbyist in Ottawa) told Max he couldn't wear his *Labatt's Blue* T-shirt because waiters could not be seen to favour one brewery over another, he was just fucking with him. They had staff shirts, baseball style with coloured sleeves, and drinking a *Brador* just before noon was the best way to start the shift.

P.E.T.

He was from the small town of Salmon Arm, which was famous for a couple of years because when Trudeau was travelling through on a train he gave protestors the finger.

Chocolate Parfait

The art critic went for a run along the river, entertaining thoughts of chucking it all in to become one of the guys selling selfie sticks in front of the Colosseum. Or the line of super dark Africans near Piazza Venezia, waiting to get their daily ration of Chanel and Gucci knock-offs. He passed a row of glass plates, mostly smashed, which covered poems by Brodski, Tolstoi, Pasolini, Joyce. At the steps up to the street, somebody'd taken a dump.

Toes

Kevin Spacey's television break was the 1980s series *Wiseguy*, which meant that Scorsese, when he adapted Henry Hill's book of the same name, had to go with *Goodfellas*. In that series, Kevin's most memorable scenes were when he took his socks off and talked to his toes. Then, in *The Usual Suspects*, walking away from the interrogation, shrugging off his limp like an actor leaving a character. But now, with asides to the audience straight out of the Bard, and the direct address to the camera at the end of s03e06 (*What're you looking at?*), Kevin has reached the pinnacle of his career. Where will he go now?

Big Smile (House of Cards Fanfic II)

Remy's great line in the previous season was when he was looking at a house in California, and there was a Luc Tuymans *catalogue raisonée* on the coffee table. "Good artist," he said, or perhaps "great artist." A line that few in the audience would have appreciated. This is why he is so wonderful, and now, as he tears his heart out listening to the Canadian actress tell him she is happy with her husband, he again has a great line: "I can't remember my last home-cooked meal."

Extra's Extra (House of Cards Fanfic III)

If she had it together, Rebecca made it to the cattle call for extras, it was an AA-type meeting, which was super ironic. She'd asked her father for money to go into a residential treatment plan, but that wasn't going to happen any time soon, so all she could do was go to meetings.

The Mortuary

The pizzeria was called that because of the marble table tops, although they stopped using marble at the mortuary a century ago. Now, stainless steel, a drain in the middle of the table, or canted to the end. A microphone hanging in the centre, a plastic bag twist-tied over the switch to protect it from blood and guts. An hour or so before they went for pizza they'd been looking at *The Dying Gaul*, in a room named for him, and he wondered, how exactly did some of these statues make it here, to the present, unscarred and unbroken, penis and ears and nose and arms and sword intact?

Not Special

Karl Ove and Michel met in the author's lounge at a writer's festival in the Canadian Rockies. Michel was fingering through the swag, muttering, herbal tea, who besides lesbians and Scandinavians drinks herbal — oh! Sorry Karl Ove, no offense. Not at all, Karl Ove said, if by *Scandinavians* you mean *Swedes*. I agree, they are disgusting with their petty-bourgeois health food habits, truly the sign of a people cut off from natural existence. At least my father, for all his faults, never sank to drinking hot water with twigs floating in it.

Special (Karl Ove and Michel, II)

You see, that's where you're the lucky one. That bitch of my mother — he pronounced it like the tree, beech — she was always trying to get me to swill that disgusting concoction *chamomile* — he pronounced it with a queer Italian-French accent, *cammo-milly*. But really, Karl Ove, Michel continued, which period of *Saturday Night Live* do you prefer, the 1970s, with those delicious impressions of Jerry Ford stumbling, or the 80s, when Eddy Murphy was their first great actor *nègre*?

Fritz

In a small provincial town, the priest had forgotten to button his top-but-one button, so his front had the curious effect of a dog collar with a gap beneath it. The police agent, who had transferred in to the region a few years earlier, was coming for confession again, and the priest dreaded these sessions. His mistress, in turn, would have the drinks waiting for him when he came by that night. The clock sounded, five or so minutes off. Maybe she'd fry him an egg.

Noli me tangere

After a hard rain, the river had overflowed its banks, so she had to run on the street, dodging taxis and scooters. He met the art historian for a coffee, they traded gossip like schoolboys do their hockey cards, *got it, got it, need it, got it.* Told it was fifteen minutes away, he hoofed it to a museum to view a couple Caravaggios, along Vittorio Massimo, up il Corso, and then, swimming against the narrative of his Blue Book, down to the Barberini. He went up the stairs — by Berini? Borromi? — and was directed by the cicerone to return to the ticket room. He came back up with his ticket and after she looked at his untorn stub, the cicerone told him to start in the rooms on the ground floor. He saw the paintings in the rooms on the ground floor, accompanied by a child in a stroller, and went up the stairs to the first floor. *Alora*, he said, *hokay*, she said, and he walked in.

Ideal Rent

He went to see Bernini's Ecstasy of Saint Theresa first, the visitor's gallery of Cardinals looking at her in the throes of passion, frozen forever in time, but when he got to the church it was closed for the siesta. He went across the street for spaghetti, came back at three with twenty minutes to kill, found a bookstore and bought a copy of the Senate report on CIA torture. Came back, learned the Bernini was being restored, walked up to the Borghese, and took a bus back to Trastevere, reading about waterboarding. Part of the issue was bubbles of air coming up the detainee's open mouths, inexperienced officers — emails from [REDACTED] asked why, if this was the most secret operation in CIA, he kept having fuck-ups sent to him, vulnerable to counter-intel, a trainwreck he was going to get off of.

Screen Grab

Mo was not too familiar with his smartphone, but his daughter had taught him how to take a shot of whatever was on the screen. One day he was sitting with Bob at the Starbucks on Main Street. Bob was complaining about what to do about his girlfriend, she was pregnant, he didn't know if they should move in together. Bob didn't know that Mo's name was short for Mohammed, he found that out about six months later, from a neighbour his girlfriend met at her pre-natal class.

Swag

Angered by the harsh conditions, women of easy virtue who were cloistered and treated at the mission in Nancy have sacked the place. – Fénéon

An *ex-prossi* made iPod holders out of felted wool. Boil the wool, or just wash it in super hot temperature. Others crocheted three remote holders on one blanket you threw over the arm of a chair you sat in when you watched TV. There was a pre-school, a hotel for weary travellers, the workshop. Before she met Agathe she'd get on the last doorway of any bus or tram & declaim Italian men and prostitution first in Italian then in English. She was still working by the train station. The odds were slim that one of her johns had a remote holder at home. He'd watch his *crimi* when he returned.

Raise the Lever of Self-esteem

The communications professor held that skimmability was a prime prerequisite in the new "infowhelm" society, quoting Wordsworth to that effect. She considered what it was to live without hope. What is hope. What did you have if you didn't have hope. His hope was buried with his husband, who left hoping, saying, the day before he [REDACTED], it will be alright, everything will be ok. A week later he went to the dentist. Afterward he would go to the hotel where his friend lived last to get his belongings. The hygienist asked him how his day was going and, his mouth open, he didn't say a word.

Partisan

Enrico put some pizza from the day before, a napkin, a novel, his notebook into a satchel and left the home, walking up a deer path behind the utility shed. The opening further up the road to another path always surprised him as he walked towards it, suddenly then, no warning of an aperture in the bush of the hi-liter green fluorescent streaks along the path itself. Mosses crumbly cling to ten-thousand-year-old rock.

Bellow

A woman on welfare with ten illegitimate children is like a professor with tenure, neither has to work for life. Except unless you count changing diapers or grading papers as work, and I certainly don't. Light stubble covering the back of his skull, wearing two shades of blue in the T-shirt and V-neck pullover that he peeled off as he settled into the hot tub. Two guys and a girl, in all-over cammo, came around the corner carrying rifles. This was in the bush near Pemberton. He asked them, you mind pointing that somewhere else?

Cold War Kids

He didn't think he had any *mansplainers* in his past, mentors
in male bloviating (or female), his father being the more
silent, his mother the *mouthy one*. But no speechifying, no
Castro-length disquisitions. They were living on a NATO
airbase in West Germany when he asked his father what
team or side they were on. He replied, There aren't sides,
words like a scalpel, not a bludgeon.

The Adjunct's August

Wearing *faux*-distressed Dad jeans (bleached thighs, boot cut) and a sprigged cowboy shirt, he sat on a couch in Bucharest, planning his itinerary for giving talks in Spain and London. On the wall was a poster for a show his friend Olga did, photographs of those killed in the late 1970s earthquake arranged in a grid of the victims' *cremains* in urns.

80s/10s

The pig-farm philosopher was concerned about his cousin, who had AIDS, or was it SADS, but he kept quiet except to offer positive comments on Facebook. The night before, he'd been in a leather bar in the West End where the hockey game played for 10 minutes with a Punjabi commentary and no one said a thing.

Coda

Have you ever accidentally eaten cat food? I mean *really* accidentally. Nothing beer and yogurt won't cure — plus granola for crunch. Plus the kid wet his sleeper when he fell asleep on my charger and I don't have any data.

SPQR

Her brow is knitted. She wears a simple dress, a soft, yellow brocade, the shoulder straps tied across the front, bow to the right. The woman looking at her, in white jeans and a pink top, Nike sneakers a technical yellow texture, tilts her head to the left, to put it on the same axis as Holofernes's.

Talking of Michelangelo (SPQR II)

After she has left, two more women walk into the room, one crosses her legs as she stands, the false gaping holes on the thigh and calf. The other tilts her head to the right.

Mark

"In the long run …" the economics professor droned on at the military college, in a lecture hall built in 1930. A wiseass from the back of the room piped up "… we'll all be dead!" That night he sat next to a literature professor, the poet, Mark Madoff. His colleague, who wore tapered shirts, was named Brodsky, which led to a few russophobic jokes. He asked him what an oak bay was. The poet had been published in *3¢ Pulp* the previous decade.

Dreams (1)

I do wish Lydia Davis would not tell us which of her stories are dreams. Such a plot spoiler, even if not true. I mean, perhaps Davis' stories aren't originally dreams, then what am I supposed to think? And what about the ones 'from Flaubert'? Like, are they from his letters? I could check at the back of Davis' book but I don't have the words.

Dreams (Snuneymuxw)

We went fishing and then my son wasn't on the plane on the way home. I was in a military office trying to find him and the soldier had written, on a small scrap of paper, in pale blue ink, *nunimo* for Nanaimo (or maybe Namao). I looked at a string of lures or hooks and saw his red one and wailed, that's supposed to be in the fish! When I told my girlfriend she said, re the hooks, shows how much I know about fishing. When I told my kid, he comforted me then brightened up: at least I was left somewhere good!

Austerity

From this time henceforth, all telephones shall be removed from their offices.

Glass Half Full

In the shed all winter the damp caused mould to grow on the barbecue, giving it a greyish-white fuzz. Luckily this softened the crud left from the last salmon bar-b-q of the season, so it only took 20 minutes to clean. When he bought the barbecue last July, they only had a floor model at the Canadian Tire, had to ride over to the warehouse a few blocks away.

Craigslist

Recently, while I was watching *Mad Max* for a second time, my girlfriend bought three pints of strawberries from a roadside stand out in the country. They were wrapped in newspaper and when my son ripped one box open he discovered the colour comics on the other side. He read them, we all did, and I noticed that the other side had ads for new and used cars and vacation properties. The newspaper was from three years earlier, before Craigslist effectively killed that revenue stream, classified ads, for newspapers.

Novel 1

When a man reads a novel about female friendship, or the relationship between two sisters, or a mother and her daughter, it is as if, travelling in a foreign country, he can suddenly understand the local language for a few weeks. Conversations take on a new and profound meaning, hitherto inexplicable actions are now comprehended. Then he finishes the book and he returns to his previous stupidity.

Novel 2

How can a novel fit inside your head? When he was running a program for the indigent it was written up by *Reader's Digest*. When he was a boy, his parents subscribed to the magazine, as well as to *Reader's Digest Condensed Books*. Five new novels appeared in one book, he remembered only one, *The Chewing Gum* or *The Bubble Gun*, a girl taking the bus across the country with only $100, it may have been written by Paul Gallico.

Pump and Dump

Balding but with a beard, in a guayabera and ragged cut-offs, Bernard crossed the shady street, twisting left with right arm under left armpit and *beeped* the truck locked. Earlier, he'd played dodge 'em cars with a guy trying to get to an ATM machine, bald with a dress shirt tucked into suit pants but no jacket.

Cheap Try Me!

Sally dug into the dregs of her Blizzard with the spoon-straw an orange that matched her hoodie. She wore it zipped up and over her head, she also had zebra tights. At the side door to the apartment building she hefted her bitch bag two or three times, the Blizzard cupped on her left. Finally the door buzzed open. A baby was crying bloody blue murder somewhere inside.

Bartending School

Local 41 of the Hospitality Employee's Union ran a week-long training program, the instructor a Chinese guy, also a magician, also had a convenience store in Fairfield. Way he saw it, it was his right to deny service to anyone, he only let three kids in the store at any one time. Keeping an eye out for shoplifters. Ice cost money he told the bartending students, don't overload the highball glass with ice. One of the students, with big hair and in a batwing sweater, was going out with a guy who would leave her to go to Japan to teach English, come back married to a Japanese woman and open a hotel in the Kootenays with money from her parents, this woman with big hair was the only one who could crack an egg with one hand. Sales rep from Carling O'Keefe came in one day, had signed on after a couple years selling lumber, couple bad years, this was when interest rates were through the roof, when asked about the boycott he didn't have a good answer. TV crew was there for the last day and one of the guys couldn't be on camera.

Coda (CB)

In the afternoon drizzle of Florence, after seeing, on a street corner, the plaque marking where British soldiers fought off retreating Germans, he ducked out of the rain into a bookstore. He walked down one wall, leafed through a few brown-edged art history books. Turned to the front of the store, in an alcove he came across an account of Chet Baker's Italian tour in the 1950s. In a "hauling coal to Newcastle" situation, as Melville wrote apropos of a German whaler borrowing lamp oil from the *Pequod*, Baker was arrested in Sicily, or was it Lucca, for possession of heroin. Five years later, he purchased a recording made by Baker in 1983, fifteen years after having his tooth cracked during a mugging in San Francisco. The record was made in Holland, and it sounded great.

Acknowledgements

Stories first drafted 2014-15 in Vienna, Italy, and Vancouver: thanks to Urban Subjects (Jeff Derksen, Sabine Bitter, Helmut Weber) for the crash pad in Ottakring. Thanks to Michael Turner and Jonathan Ball, to Robyn Laba and Chris Power, to Mark Laba, Julie Sawatsky, Devon Burnham, and to anyone else who first read these as screenshots on Twitter and Instagram. Thanks to Kevin Chong and *Joyland*, to Chris Brayshaw and CSA Space, and to Stuart Ross and Proper Tales Press, for showing earlier versions. Thank you to Stephen Waddell for the cover photograph, which captures, for me, the "Vancouver to Italy and back" feel of these stories, a dynamic that also harkens to earlier works by George Bowering and Ian Wallace. Thanks to Chris Brayshaw for the author photo, taken the day of the fire at Main and Broadway in October, 2020. Thank you to Kevin Chong and to Anakana Schofield for generous blurbs. Thanks to Brian, Clint, and the Anvil crew for their work on the book.

About the author

Clint Burnham was born in Comox, British Columbia, which is on the traditional territory of the K'ómoks (Sathloot) First Nation, centred historically on kwaniwsam. Since 1995 he has lived in the Mount Pleasant district of Vancouver, on the traditional ancestral territories of the Coast Salish peoples, including traditional territories of the Squamish (Sḵwxwú7mesh Úxwumixw), Tsleil-Waututh (səlilwətaʔɬ), Musqueam (xʷməθkʷəy̓əm), and Kwikwetlem (kʷikʷəƛ̓əm) Nations. Books include *Airborne Photo* (stories, 1999), *Smoke Show* (novel, 2005), *Rental Van* (poetry, 2007),*The Benjamin Sonnets* (poetry, 2009), and *Pound @ Guantánamo* (poetry, 2016). He has taught at the University of British Columbia, Emily Carr Institute of Art and Design, Capilano College, and, since 2007, at Simon Fraser University.